For Sally

P. P. & H. C.

• First U.S. edition 2013 • Library of Congress Catalog Card Number 2012947755 • ISBN 978-0-7636-6314-8 • Printed in Dongguan, Guangdong, China • This book was typeset in Quercus. • The illustrations were done in pencil and watercolor. • Candlewick Press • 99 Dover Street • Somerville, Massachusetts 02144 • visit us at www.candlewick.com • 13 14 15 16 17 18 TLF 10 9 8 7 6 5 4 3 2 1

Amy's Three Best Things

Philippa Pearce

illustrated by

Helen Craig

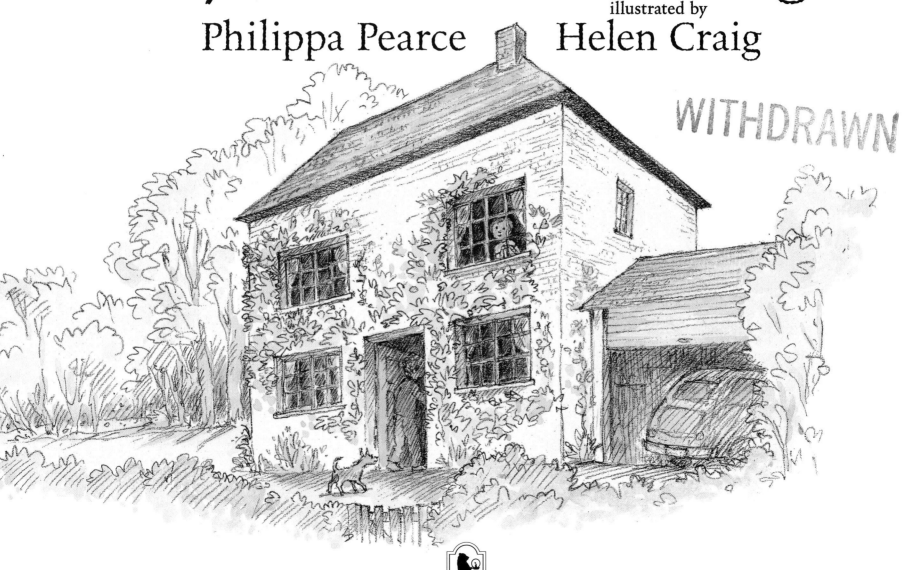

CANDLEWICK PRESS

One day Amy said,

"I'd like to go and see Grandma soon. I'd like to go all by myself, and I'd like to stay the night."

Her mother said, "Are you sure, Amy?" For Amy had not been away from home by herself before.

"Of course I'm sure," Amy said. "In fact, I'll stay two nights. No, I'll stay three."

Amy packed her bag with her teddy bear and her pajamas and all the other ordinary things she needed. Then she put in three more things. One thing came from the floor beside her bed, another thing came from the mantel in her bedroom,

and the third thing came from the rack over the bathtub.

Those are my three best things for a visit, she thought.

"What will you do while I'm away?" Amy asked her mother.

"Well, this evening I have to cut the grass," her mother said.

"What will Bill and Bonzo be doing?"

"Bill will be in bed. Asleep, I hope. Bonzo will be somewhere chewing a stick."

"I just wanted to know," said Amy.

At Grandma's house, Amy unpacked her bag. But she didn't take out her three best things, because they were secret. She and Grandma spent the rest of the afternoon spring-cleaning Grandma's old toy cupboard. Amy found it extremely interesting. Then it was time for supper and bed.

Amy soon fell asleep, but later she woke. It was still daylight. She missed her mother and Bill and Bonzo. She wanted her own home.

Then she remembered her three best things. She got out of bed and fetched the first one: a little stripy mat from the floor beside her bed at home.

Amy laid the mat on the floor by her bed in Grandma's house. She sat on the edge of the bed with her feet on the mat.

At first Amy didn't feel any better. Then she noticed a tingling in her feet. She stood up on the mat. It seemed to shift beneath her. She sat down on the mat only just in time, for it was beginning to move.

The mat was rising, slowly at first. Then, in a rush, it rose much higher. It flew toward the window, and the window opened and Amy, on her magic mat, sailed out into the summer air.

The mat flew smoothly and fast in the direction of home. And there was her house, and there was the yard, and her mother had just finished mowing the lawn. She was scolding Bonzo, who had chewed up a stick all over the fresh-cut grass.

Then Amy wanted to see what Bill was doing, and the mat took her to his bedroom window. There was Bill asleep in his crib with his knitted rabbit held up to his cheek.

Amy wasn't feeling unhappy anymore. The mat turned and carried her back as swiftly as before — back to her grandma's house, in through the window, and down to the floor by Amy's bed.

It was just an ordinary little stripy mat again.

The next day Amy and her grandma had a picnic lunch in the park, and Grandma bought ice cream to finish off the lunch. The sun shone, and Amy went to the playground and swung and climbed and slid and twirled. They came back late and tired.

That night, Amy fell asleep quickly, but moonlight on her face woke her. She sat up, missing home all over again. She missed her mother and Bill and Bonzo.

Then she remembered her three best things. She got out of bed and fetched the second one: a tiny wooden horse from her mantel at home.

Amy put the tiny horse on the floor, and at once it began to grow. As it grew, it pawed the ground and snorted with impatience.

When the horse was the right size, Amy climbed onto its back. The horse set off at a gallop through the air — out of the window and into the moonshiny night. It whinnied for joy as it rushed toward Amy's house.

As late as this, everyone would
be indoors. Amy looked into
the living room. There sat her
mother, watching television, with
Bonzo snoozing at her feet. In his
bedroom, Bill was also asleep, with
his knitted rabbit at his cheek.

And now the horse tossed
its mane and set off back to
Grandma's house. It galloped all
the way and in through Amy's
window and down to her bedside.

Then it was just a tiny wooden
horse again. Amy picked it up and
put it safely on the mantel.

The next day Amy and her grandma stayed indoors because it rained. They made a cake together. It was a splendid cake and a large one. They frosted it, and Amy decorated it with sugar flowers and jelly beans and colored sprinkles.

"Perfect for tomorrow," said Grandma, "when your mother comes with Bill and Bonzo to take you home. There'll be a fair in town, too, and we could all go together before you leave."

"I'd like that," said Amy. "I'd like that very much. And then, after the fair, I'll say good-bye to you and I'll get in the car with the others and I'll go home."

"That's right," said Grandma.

That night Amy fell asleep to the sound of rain. Later, thunder and lightning woke her. She sat up, thinking what a long way off tomorrow seemed. She wanted her mother and Bill and Bonzo *now*.

Then she remembered her three best things. She got out of bed and fetched the third one: a little wooden boat from the bathroom at home.

As she looked, the boat began to grow, then to rock as though it were riding on water. When it was big enough, Amy stepped in. The boat rose and sailed out through the window and into the stormy night. Amy was not afraid of the storm, and the rain did not even get her pajamas wet.

Through the whistling winds and rushing rain, the boat took Amy to her home. She looked in through the living-room window, but the television was switched off. There was no one there, not even Bonzo. No one was in Bill's room either. His crib was empty.

At last Amy looked in the garage and—as she had feared—the car was gone. Then she knew that all her family had gone away without her. She flung herself down in the bottom of the boat and cried.

The boat swung around and started off the way it had come. It took Amy back to her grandma's house and in through the window, and then it was just a little bathtub boat again on the floor. Amy stood beside it and cried and cried.

From downstairs Amy heard the sound of people talking: Grandma had visitors. But Amy did not care if they heard her. From downstairs, someone — it wasn't her grandma — said, "Hush!" Then, quite clearly, Amy heard her mother's voice: "It's Amy crying!" Then there were footsteps hurrying upstairs and the bedroom door was flung open and her mother was kneeling beside her, asking, "Amy, whatever is the matter?"

"I missed you all," said Amy, still crying because she couldn't stop at once.

"Well, here we all are," said her mother. "We came tonight instead of tomorrow." She tucked Amy in and kissed her good night.

"Tomorrow, if it's nice outside, we'll go to the fair."

And the next day the sun shone, so they all went to the fair.

Amy's favorite thing at the fair was the old-fashioned merry-go-round. When the music played, all the animals moved up and down and around in their big circle.

Amy chose to ride a dragon. When the music started, she clung on tight and waved good-bye to her family. Then the merry-go-round swirled her off so that she could no longer see them. But she knew they would still be there when she came around again.

Bill was laughing and waving both hands, and Amy waved back.

Around and around went the merry-go-round with Amy on her dragon, and sometimes she saw her family and sometimes she didn't.

But they were always there.